The Adventures of Itty Bitty Kitty ™

Library of Congress Cataloging-in-Publication Data

Keeshan, Robert.
Just right for Itty Bitty Kitty / by Bob Keeshan ; illustrations by Jane Maday.
p.   cm
"TV's Captain Kangaroo"—Cover.
Summary: When the hotel manager orders Itty Bitty Kitty out, the other employees
try to find her a home, but it seems that the hotel is where she belongs.
ISBN 1-57749-019-3
1. Cats—Juvenile fiction. [1. Cats—Fiction. 2. Hotels, motels, etc.—Fiction.]
I. Maday, Jane, ill. II. Title.
PZ10.3.K246Ju 1997
[E]—dc20   96-41672

First printing
Printed in Singapore

02 01 00 99 98   7 6 5 4 3 2 1

For a current catalog of Fairview Press titles,
please call this toll-free number: 1-800-544-8207.

Produced by Mega-Books, Inc.
Design and art direction by Nutshell Design, Inc.

Publisher's Note: Fairview Press publishes books and other materials related to
the subjects of family and social issues. Its publications, including *Just Right for
Itty Bitty Kitty,* do not necessarily reflect the philosophy of
Fairview Hospital and Healthcare Services or their treatment programs.

Just Right for
Itty Bitty Kitty

by Bob Keeshan

illustrations by Jane Maday

Fairview Press
Minneapolis, Minnesota

*To a friend and colleague who has unselfishly dedicated
her life to animals and, through them, touched many people's
lives in very special ways. Ruth Mary Manecke has raised,
rehabilitated, and loved animals from the time she was a
small child. She has shared her expert zoological knowledge
as well as her respect for nature and the environment with
millions of children and parents through her work at the
Bronx Zoo and her role in supplying all the animals on
Captain Kangaroo. Ruth's sensitivity was a great
encouragement in the creation of Itty Bitty Kitty and her
many adventures. I thank her for her love of animals and
her ability to see a twinkle in the eye of this and every
homeless creature among us.*

— B.K.

For John, the best husband ever.

— J.M.

   One morning Itty Bitty Kitty woke up and yawned. She
jumped off the chair she'd slept on and stre-e-e-etched her
front legs. Then she stre-e-e-etched her back legs. She
trotted across the hotel lobby and through the dining room,
where the tables were set for breakfast. She scratched on
the swinging door to the kitchen and meowed.

"Well," Esmeralda said as she opened the door, "if it isn't Itty Bitty Kitty, ready for her breakfast." The waitress took a carton of milk out of the refrigerator, poured some in a saucer, and placed it on the floor.

Itty Bitty Kitty tried it, but it was too cold.

"Give me that milk," said Pierre, the chef. He heated the milk, then poured it back into the saucer.

Itty Bitty Kitty tried it, but it was too hot.

"I know what she'll like," said Jeannie, another waitress.
She added some milk from one of the small pitchers she
had ready for the dining room tables.

Itty Bitty Kitty tried it. Ahh! Just right. She drank the milk
and licked her whiskers.

Jeannie let Itty Bitty Kitty out of the kitchen and went back to work. The little kitten stopped in the dining room to wash her face.

The side door opened, and Mr. Dunhoffer, the hotel manager, walked in. Itty Bitty Kitty did not see him, but Mr. Dunhoffer saw her.

"What is that cat doing in here?" he bellowed. Mr. Dunhoffer did not like cats, especially in his hotel.

Esmeralda, Jeannie, and Pierre came running from the kitchen. Justin, one of the bellhops, came running from the lobby. Mr. Dunhoffer grabbed Itty Bitty Kitty, but she slipped through his fingers, circled Justin, and raced out of the dining room.

"I don't know what that cat is doing in my hotel," said Mr. Dunhoffer, "but I want it found, and I want it out of here. Today!"

"Yes, sir," chorused the staff as the manager stomped out.

"How can he be so mean?" asked Esmeralda. "Nobody minds having that kitten around."

"Mr. Dunhoffer does," said Justin, "and that's all that counts, I guess."

"I'd take her home with me," said Jeannie, "but my daughter's allergic to cats."

Esmeralda couldn't take her because her landlord didn't allow pets. Pierre couldn't take her because his poodle, Mimi, hated cats.

"I know," said Justin. "I'll take her to my mother's house. She's always adopting stray animals."

Meanwhile, Itty Bitty Kitty was hiding in the closet where the hotel employees changed into their work clothes.

She climbed onto a briefcase. It was much too hard.

She jumped onto a garment bag. It was much too soft.

Near a locker, an open gym bag sat on a bench. The kitten crawled in and curled up on a sweatshirt. Ahh! Just right. Itty Bitty Kitty settled down to take a catnap.

Itty Bitty Kitty slept for a long time. She slept so soundly she did not hear someone come in and change into the clothes that had been hanging in the locker. She did not even feel the gym bag move when that same someone picked it up.

Kerplunk! The bag was dropped, and there was a loud bang. Itty Bitty Kitty woke up. It was very dark. A car engine started. The kitten felt herself moving. She scratched at the inside of the bag, but she couldn't get out. She meowed loudly, but nobody came.

At last the car stopped. The frightened kitten heard the trunk lid pop up. *Meow!* she cried. *Meow!*

The zipper opened, and there was Justin! "So that's where you were! We looked all over for you," he said. "Well, since you're here, I might as well skip the gym and take you right to Mom's."

Justin moved the tiny kitten to the front seat and drove away.

Itty Bitty Kitty was fascinated by the car. First she helped Justin steer, then she climbed over his shoulder and jumped into the back. She hunched down on the shelf by the rear window and watched to make sure that the car behind didn't get too close.

When they got to his mother's house, Justin carried Itty Bitty Kitty inside. "Look what I brought you, Mom," he said, handing her the kitten.

"Oh, how cute," his mom said. "I'd love to keep her." She put the kitten down on the floor and walked outside with Justin.

Itty Bitty Kitty looked around and began to explore.

Woof! Woof! A huge hairy dog bounded into the living room.

Itty Bitty Kitty ran behind the sofa.

Hiss! spat the big striped cat crouching there.

Itty Bitty Kitty ran into the kitchen, the dog and the cat close behind. "Look out!" squawked a parrot sitting on the back of a chair, flapping its wings.

A tough-looking gray cat with only one ear looked up from its saucer of milk. *Grrr!* The cat swatted Itty Bitty Kitty and the kitten went flying.

Itty Bitty Kitty landed on her feet. She raced through the
dining room, the dog and two cats right behind her.
Yap! Yap! Yap! Two small dogs not much bigger than the
kitten jumped off a dining room chair and joined the chase.

Itty Bitty Kitty ran for the front door. She leaped onto the screen and scrambled up as high as she could.

Woof! Woof! Grrr! Hiss! Yap! Yap! Yap! Hiss! Woof! Woof!

"Oh, dear," said Justin's mother. She opened the screen door and scooped the shaking kitten into her arms. "I don't think this is going to work."

"You're right," said Justin. "I'll take her to my apartment."

The next day Justin went to work and left Itty Bitty Kitty by herself. She explored his apartment, but since it had only one very neat room and a bathroom, there wasn't much to see.

She sat on the windowsill and watched the birds. She played with the toy Justin had given her. She drank some of her water. She sharpened her claws on the sofa bed and stretched.

After she ran out of things to do, she curled up in the bathroom sink for a catnap.

When Justin came home, Itty Bitty Kitty wouldn't let him alone for a minute. She rubbed up against his legs, purring loudly. She raced around the apartment on top of the furniture. She helped Justin eat his supper.

After they finished eating, Itty Bitty Kitty climbed up on Justin's lap.

"I'll bet you were lonesome, weren't you?" he said, scratching her behind the ears. "My mom's place was too crowded with other animals. This place is too empty. The hotel is just right for you."

In the morning, Justin smuggled Itty Bitty Kitty back into the hotel in his gym bag. He sneaked her into the kitchen, where Jeannie, Esmeralda, and Pierre welcomed her back with milk and shrimp. Later, Jeannie carried her to Maria, who hid the kitten in her housekeeping cart.

But while the maid wasn't looking, Itty Bitty Kitty slipped away. She scampered down the hallway and around the corner into the lobby. She jumped up onto her favorite chair in front of the fireplace to take a catnap. Ahh! Just right.

At that moment, Mr. Dunhoffer walked in with his granddaughter, Jenny.

"Justin!" Mr. Dunhoffer hollered. "I thought you got rid of that animal!"

"I did, Mr. Dunhoffer," Justin began, "but . . ."

"Oooh, she's so cute," cooed Jenny as she scratched Itty Bitty Kitty's furry belly. "Grandpa, how can you be mean to this little kitty?"

"See, Mr. Dunhoffer?" said Justin. "Everybody loves having her around."

"I do not," said Mr. Dunhoffer. "Besides, Jenny is only a little girl."

"That sure is a sweet kitten," said a guest who was checking in. "She gives the hotel a real homey feeling."

"But . . . ," said Mr. Dunhoffer.

"Please let her stay, Grandpa," said Jenny. "Come on, please, please, pretty please?"

"Very well," said Mr. Dunhoffer grudgingly. "She can stay here for now."

So Itty Bitty Kitty got to stay in the hotel that was just right for her. At least until Mr. Dunhoffer's granddaughter went home.